DESTINATION DISASTER

For Jeremy, March 1998
and for Class 3–9 at Melville High School

Contents

Chapter One

Important facts about me: James Harris.

1. I hate being called Jimmy.

2. I'm twelve years old.

3. I can't spell for peanuts and this drives my grandfather (I call him "Pa") wild.

4. I'm into skateboarding, and that drives him wild, too. He's into football, hunting, fishing, baseball, and spelling. Yes, spelling.

5. I'm skinny and short for my age. I have brown hair and brown eyes. My mom is always telling me that I'm going to start growing soon, but I'm still small enough to climb out of the small window in my bedroom whenever Pa comes over and starts talking about how he wants to take me to some football game, or phones up and asks me to come and watch a baseball game with him.

6. My mother is cool. She's a computer expert, and she often goes away to conferences and stuff. The downside of that is she always wants

me to stay with Pa and Grandma, and I always want to stay with one of my friends. We usually make a deal so that she gets her way 90% of the time and I get my way about 10%, or at least that's what it feels like. I moaned so much that she wrote it all down, and it turned out I got my way 55% of the time and she got her way 45%.

7. My father died climbing a mountain when I was three. I don't remember him, but I figure he must've been a lot like Pa – big and tall and powerful and good at all the stuff Pa likes.

So those are the facts, and here's the story of what happened to Pa and me during my first month at junior high school.

It was the hottest September for about a million years. The weather had been windy and cold most of the summer, and the day we started school, it suddenly turned hot and sunny and stayed that way. Our classrooms were like barbecues.

I dragged myself home from school one day to find Mom at home, chucking things into a suitcase.

I flopped down on her bedroom floor. "Water!" I gasped.

She stepped over me. "Hi, Jim. Pack your gear. You're going to have to stay with Pa and Grandma for a week. There's a huge emergency, and I have to go to Los Angeles."

"I'll come, too," I said, finding the energy to sit up. There was surfing there, and I could probably just hang out on the beach all day.

Yeah, right! Mom didn't even bother to respond to that suggestion. Of course, I started to argue the merits of my case, but I could tell right from the start that I wasn't going to win this one.

"Oh! I nearly forgot," Mom said. "Pa's going to take you fishing."

"I don't want to go fishing."

She sat on her bed and rubbed her forehead tiredly. "Look, Jim – just do it, all right? He thinks it'll be good for you."

"You mean it will make a man out of me," I said with a scowl.

"Whatever. It's something he's wanted to do for ages. You'll miss some school, but it's so hot you're probably not learning anything anyway."

Great. Just what I like. Having my life turned upside-down and I don't even get asked about it.

"Go and pack," Mom said. "I have to leave in half an hour, so move it!"

I started tossing things in the backpack Pa had given me for my birthday, even though I'd told him I wanted a new portable computer game. I put the essentials in first: Walkman, chocolate bars, baseball cap. Then I threw in sneakers, a sweatshirt, some shorts, four T-shirts, socks, clean underwear. Hairbrush, toothbrush, toothpaste, soap. The cell phone. Spare batteries for my Walkman. My old computer game that I could do with my eyes shut. You know, the essentials.

Mom came bustling in. She gave me a quick hug. "Thanks for not pitching a fit, Jim. I only found out I had to go about an hour ago."

I thought I had pitched a fit. Next time I'd have to crank it up a notch or two.

She gave my gear an expert, mother-type look. "Throw in a sleeping bag. Bathing trunks. Towel. Air mattress."

"Trunks?" I said. "You mean there's water? I can swim?"

"There's generally water when you go fishing," my mother said.

Yeah. Well. I just hadn't put the two together. I crammed in my brightest Hawaiian print trunks.

She drove me to Grandma and Pa's house and gave me a huge hug. "Have fun. Don't get lost."

"Mom!" I said desperately. "I don't want to go fishing! I don't want to spend three days alone with Pa."

She held my shoulders. "Jim, it'll be okay. Just remember that he really does love you."

Then she was gone. I picked up my gear and started up their front walk. It was all very well for her to say that he loved me. It didn't feel like he loved me. I couldn't think of a single thing about me that he even liked.

He for sure didn't like my packing. "You won't pick up as much as a squeak on either of those," he said, pointing at the Walkman and cell phone. He snorted at the chocolate bars. "They'll melt and they'll be extra weight, but if you want them, you carry them." He just about had a fit at the clean underwear. "Take 'em out, Jimmy lad! What are you? Some weak chunk of marshmallow that can't wear the same undies for three days?" He got to the trunks and towel, and his eyebrows climbed into his hair. "Now these are interesting. We're not going to some beach resort. What's wrong with swimming in your shorts? And the sun will dry you just as well as any fluffy towel will." He took out two of the T-shirts, too. He threw my soap and toothpaste out along with my hairbrush and the computer game. "You'll survive without all that, Jimmy. It's all extra weight. Mark my words, you'll be glad you don't have them after we've been walking a few hours."

"I hope we're going far enough out that we don't see anybody else," I said. "We're going to stink by the time we're done with this."

Pa's eyebrows twitched together, but he decided to make a joke of it. "Smelling bad is the smartest thing we can do if we get lost. That way, the bloodhounds will be able to find us more easily if they need to."

He wanted me to leave my air mattress behind, too. I didn't say anything, but when he'd packed everything back up, I strapped it on along with my sleeping bag. I also put my game back in.

While he fiddled with his own gear and loaded everything in the car, I phoned my friend John.

"You are so lucky!" he gasped when I told him.

"Yeah," I said. "Think of me when you're happily sitting in school. I'll be lost somewhere in the wild, with just a crazy grandfather for company."

"But think of it!" John gasped. "You're going into the wild! You could get mixed up with a ring of hunters poaching out of season, you know, like up around Lake Tahoe last week." He was all wound up. "I saw it on television – helicopters and guns and police all over the place."

"I don't think so, John," I said. "The only action I'm likely to see is when Pa explodes

11

because I can't keep up with him." Still, it made me feel a little better that he was so jealous.

We got in the car. Pa was bouncing around like a kid. "We're going to have such a great time, Jimmy! Just you and me. You'll love it – just like your father used to."

It'd be a miracle if we loved anything – including each other – by the time we finished. And because I've never actually seen a miracle happen, I wasn't holding my breath.

Grandma drove us to wherever it was we were going. "How long till we get there?" I asked.

The road was full of hills and I was feeling carsick.

"Only a couple more hours," Pa said cheerfully.

I lay down on the back seat and tried to die. Pa never got carsick and he acted like it was all my fault and I could stop it if I really wanted to. In his world, only weak people got carsick.

We stayed in a lodge-type of motel that night in a settlement that was so small I didn't even think it could be called a one-horse town. In the morning we drove up the narrowest, windiest road in the universe for another hour.

"Here we are, Jimmy!" Pa cried.

I sat up slowly and peered out of the window. "Here" consisted of a road that stopped at a fence and a ragged looking path that straggled up the hill behind it.

Pa dumped our stuff out on the grass. His pack was huge, like him. He had the tent and his waders. I wanted to make a crack about how only weak people needed waders and that tough guys like me stood in rivers in basic bathing trunks, but I didn't want to make him mad so I shut up.

Grandma handed me the lunch bag. "Don't drop it," Pa said. "From here on in, we only eat what we catch."

I hitched my bag over my shoulder and hoped he was joking.

Chapter Two

We set off up the path, with Pa in front taking huge steps, and me tagging along behind. "Your father loved this hike," Pa called back over his shoulder. "He used to run the whole way – I could never keep up with him."

Thanks, Pa. That's just what I needed to know.

After ten minutes, Pa was out of sight. "Great," I said to a passing butterfly. "What if I get lost? What if I fall down and sprain my ankle?"

I struggled to the top of a hill and looked down the path ahead of me. Pa was collapsed on the ground, face down. I raced down the slope.

"Pa! Pa! What happened? Are you okay?" I was panicked – what was I going to do if he wasn't all right? He was so big I'd never be able to move him.

He sat up just as I reached him. "Of course I'm all right, Jimmy. Why wouldn't I be?"

I sank to my knees, gasping. "Why wouldn't you be? Maybe because people sprawled face down in the daisies don't usually get up in a hurry."

"I was resting," he said, "since it takes you so darned long to get anywhere."

"You try it on my legs," I growled. "They're half as long as yours."

He didn't answer that. "Anyway, what would you have done if I had collapsed?"

What was this – test Jim for emergency ability? No way, Pa. I leaned over and picked a yellow flower. "I'd have done this." I put the flower on his chest, jumped to my feet and said, "Two, four, six, eight, dig in and don't wait!"

He chuckled. "Thanks a lot! So, instead of a normal eulogy, you'd just take my collapse as an excuse to eat something? You'd have to be a real worm to do that at a funeral."

"Well, that's how you make me feel. Like a worm," I muttered, not really caring if he heard.

It wasn't a good start to the expedition in my opinion. Why couldn't Pa just accept that I was a huge disappointment and let me get on with my life? My skateboarding, bad spelling, air-mattress enjoying, short-legged life.

We walked forever – up hills, along hills, down hills, and around hills. Sometimes we were in the

16

forest, and sometimes we were in ferns and bushes and stuff that grew over my head so I couldn't see where we were going. Sometimes there was a small path, but I knew I'd never find my way out of there without Pa. I wished I'd kept the cell phone.

To keep myself going, every time we climbed yet another hill and plodded through yet another valley, I searched for a rock face or cliff and pretended that I was halfway up it and Pa was at the bottom, freaking out. I think about the only way I'm like my father is that I like to climb stuff. Pa, of course, isn't interested in encouraging my natural born climbing ability.

Just when I was sure I couldn't walk another step, he stopped in the shade of a tree and waited for me. "Feel like some lunch, Jimmy?"

I sank to the ground. "Do I ever!"

He handed me a water bottle. "I'll say this for you, boy – you're not a whiner."

Gee, thanks, Pa.

We ate Grandma's bacon, lettuce, and tomato sandwiches, a couple of apples, and some cookies.

"Make the most of it," said Pa. "It'll be raw stuff for us for the next three days."

"You're joking!" I said.

"Nope." He snapped off a grass stem beside him. "Look at how dry everything is. There's a total fire ban in this area."

I stared at him, but his mouth didn't even twitch. I wondered if I could last for three days on chocolate bars and river water. There was no way I was going to eat raw fish.

"Do you hear that?" Pa asked.

"Yeah," I said. "It's a helicopter. What about it?"

"They're fire watching," he said. "If we light a fire, we're dead meat."

"Cooked or raw?" I asked.

He gave me a glance from under the hedges that he calls his eyebrows. His eyes sparkled a bit, but he didn't say anything. I wondered whether to tell him John's idea about out-of-season poachers and helicopters chasing them, but I decided not to.

Then we got to our feet and started walking again. There was no way in the world I was going to ask him how far it was. I just knew my father would never ever have asked a question like that. I pretended we wouldn't get there until it had been dark for an hour so I'd have a nice surprise if we got there sooner. And if we got there later than that I'd be so tired I wouldn't care anyway.

It was about two hours later when Pa stopped on top of yet another hill while I struggled up toward him. He yelled, "Here we are, Jimmy! What do you think of that!" He waved his hand out in front of him.

I stared. "That" was the first river we'd seen all day. It lay below us, sparkling and bright like the tail of a sky-rocket gleaming through the night. "Wow!" I whispered. "That is awesome!"

Pa looked pleased. "Go ahead and take a swim, Jimmy. You probably feel like one by now."

"Yahoo!" I yelled and belted down the hill. I dumped my pack, stripped down to my trunks – which I'd worn under my clothes all day in anticipation of this exact moment – and jumped into the river. I lay on my back and floated in the current. It was cool and so clear that when I flipped over I could see the stones on the bottom. Ferns grew along the banks, and straggly trees let the sunlight in so that it dappled the water.

Pa tramped down the hill. "Are you coming in, Pa?" I yelled.

He shook his head. "Rivers are for fishing, not swimming." But he gave me a grin. "When I was your age I swam, too, but not now."

"You want me to help you put up the tent?" I asked, coming up from a duck dive.

"No hurry," he said. "You can do it yourself when you get out. Right now, I'm going to have some coffee."

Made with cold water? While I was thinking that sounded gross, he rummaged in his pack and dragged out a little gas burner. "It doesn't count as a fire," he said, not even cracking a smile. "Doesn't spark. Doesn't leave embers."

So he did have a sense of humor, did he?

He came down to the water to fill up the pot.

He looked over at me and said, "There's an eel following you."

"Very funny, Pa. You're not catching me twice."

He dipped the pot in the water. "Oh well, their bites don't hurt too much, I guess."

"Huh!" I said and turned on my back so I couldn't see him.

Something brushed my ankle, then my knee. I shrieked and kicked and splashed. If it was an eel I

didn't want it thinking that my bright, floral trunks were some sort of a snack. My feet hit the stones on the bottom and I got myself out of the water fast.

"Told you," said Pa. He lay back, leaning against his pack. "I guess that'll be the last swim you'll have."

"The last swim in these." I said. "I guess from here on out my shorts will be fine. There's no point in wearing a fluorescent sign that says, 'Eel Food.'"

His eyebrows wriggled and again, his eyes sparkled. It'd be kind of nice to know if he thought that was funny or dumb. Was it weak or strong to try to discourage eels from inviting you for lunch, if you get my drift?

I lay in the sun and dried out while we waited for the water to boil. This was the life. Suddenly, I felt sorry for John and all the others stuck in a baking hot classroom back at school.

As soon as I was all dried off, Pa helped me put up the tent.

"Why don't you get a new one?" I asked. "This canvas thing is really heavy, and it doesn't even have its own groundsheet. The new ones weigh just about nothing, and they're all in one piece. They keep out the bugs, too."

Pa grunted. "This one's good enough for me. I used it when I took your father fishing when he was a nipper like you."

I sat back on my heels. "What was my dad like?"

Pa pounded a stake in with the head of a little hatchet. "He was the best darned football player that I ever saw. A natural fisherman. A top-class sportsman."

So tell me stuff I don't know. Like did he ever do anything that made you mad? There were times when I hated my father.

We got the tent up. I unrolled my air mattress. It was one of those fancy ones that practically inflates itself – you just have to give it a few puffs. "Huh!" Pa snorted. "Weak!" He threw his sleeping bag onto the bare groundsheet.

"I'm going swimming," I said, glaring at him.

"Suit yourself. But go downstream, will you, so you don't bother the fish. I'm going to take the rod out in a minute."

At least he didn't tell me to be careful in case I drowned.

I put on my most neutral shorts and messed around in the river for the rest of the afternoon. It would have been perfect if John had been with me, but you can't have everything. The river was great. It mostly came up to the tops of my legs and ran swiftly over stones, but every so often there was a place where it ran into a deep pool. I'd swim a while, then lie on a rock to warm up again. My favorite rock was a big one right out in the middle of the river. I lay on it and dangled my feet in the water.

I went back to our camp when I got hungry. We'd pitched the tent pretty close to the river on a narrow strip of flat land between the water and the hill. The ground was covered with dry grass and small scrubby trees that bent in the direction the river was traveling. I looked at them thoughtfully. I wouldn't want to be around here in a flood.

There was no sign of Pa, so I carefully divided the last of the sandwiches and ate my share. I was getting cold. I hung my damp shorts on a branch, pulled on some warmer clothes, and went back to watching the river. Today really hadn't been so bad. I hadn't died on the hike getting here. The river was a piece of paradise and it looked like it'd be pretty easy to keep out of Pa's way for the next two days. It'd be okay.

I turned and looked at the tent. I hoped he didn't snore.

The sun was going down when he came back and I was hungry again. He came striding through the water, his dark green waders shining in the remaining light. He carried a fish in a net over his shoulder and he had a satisfied grin on his face.

We had fried fish and rice for dinner. I thought the fish was pretty tasteless, but I was hungry so I ate it.

"I don't know about you, Jimmy, but I'm just about tuckered out," he said when we'd washed the dishes in the river. "I'm turning in for the night." And then the snoring began.

Chapter Three

I felt like I'd just fallen asleep when he was yanking on the bottom of my sleeping bag. "Up you go, Jimmy! It's a perfect morning and we're going fishing."

I clutched the sleeping bag tighter around me. "Uh, that's okay, Pa. Go ahead. I'll come later."

The next thing I knew, I was in a heap on the grass and the sleeping bag was swinging gently from a branch. "Rise and shine, Jimmy. Rise and shine." He towered above me, looking as big as a dinosaur. I rose, but I can't say I was shining. Morning is definitely not my best time.

We had cereal for breakfast with milk that I'd made by shaking up powder with water. It was disgusting, but I choked it down because Pa's eyes were on me and I knew that any second he was going to tell me I was weak.

We headed up the river. He'd brought along a rod for me. "This was your dad's," he said. He held it as carefully as if it were made of gold.

Holding that rod gave me a funny feeling. I was all mixed up, like I wanted to keep it forever, but at the same time I wanted to smash it to pieces and watch it float down the river. I walked behind him, trying to keep up with his big steps. I was wearing one of my two T-shirts, some shorts, and half a bottle of sunscreen, but he was dressed in a heap of thick gear and he had his huge waders over the top of everything. They were rubber gumboots at the bottom and some nylon stuff was joined to them so that they looked like a pair of overalls with rubber feet. If our tent got washed away in a flood we could probably live for weeks in his waders. The water was around his knees, but I had to struggle because it came up to my waist most of the time.

He was across the river and organizing his line by the time I got there.

"What took you so long?" he asked, raising his big bushy eyebrows at me.

"I'm still asleep," I grumbled.

"Humph," he said and grabbed my fishing rod.

I collapsed on the grass and tried to get the circulation back into my feet while he fiddled with the line.

"Right, Jimmy," he said, wading into the river. "Here's what you do." He pulled out some line, held it looped in one hand, and flicked the rod, releasing a little more line with each flick. With the final flick, he let go the last of the line coiled in his hand. It landed quietly on the water and sank into the depths of the pool.

He turned to me. "Think you can do that?"

It looked dead easy. "Sure, Pa. No sweat." I looked at the rod that my father had used. That rod had probably caught a thousand fish. Pa reeled the line back in and gave it to me.

I took it and flicked it, just the way Pa had. You have no idea how big a mess one person can make of a fishing rod and a length of skinny line, but believe me, it's impressive.

I didn't look at Pa, but my shoulders were tensed as I waited for him to yell at me.

He didn't. He just took the line and untangled it. "Try again, Jimmy," he said. "Watch carefully."

I watched more carefully than a cat watches a bird, but still when I flicked, the line got tangled. It happened again and again. I kept thinking he'd given me a useless line, but every time I messed up, he would show me what to do, and the line would flick out sweetly across the water.

I gritted my teeth and tried again and again. My legs were freezing and I was just waiting for Pa to start telling me how my father never messed up, even once – but he didn't. He was so patient it was making me nervous.

"Great Scott, Jimmy!" he bellowed suddenly. "Why didn't you say you were cold? Look at you! You can't flick the line when you can't keep your hands still."

I hadn't actually noticed. I looked at my hands and they were shaking with cold.

"Get out!" Pa yelled. "Go and lie in the sun for a while."

I staggered out of the water. My feet were white and my knees were blue. I would have given a lot right then to have my big towel Pa had chucked out at home. He tugged his sweatshirt off. "Put that on, son." He sounded cross, as if it was my fault I was cold.

I sat on the bank and watched him. It looked so easy. A flick of the wrist and the line snaked out, hovered over the water, and dropped gently onto it.

He fished, while I concentrated on getting my blood back to the right temperature. I watched him. It looked so easy. I think I went to sleep for a few minutes because the next thing I knew, Pa was standing beside me, dripping.

"How about something warm to drink, Jimmy?" He'd brought the gas burner, the pot, and some of Grandma's cookies, too. It's amazing how hungry making a mess of a fishing line can make you.

When he'd finished his mug of coffee, he said, "Okay. Time to try again."

I took his sweatshirt off slowly. I didn't want to try again. Why couldn't he just face it? I wasn't a natural sportsman.

I took the rod and waded out into the pool. I flicked my wrist and the line rolled out across the water and settled gently, just the way it had done with Pa. I forgot to be quiet and still. "I did it!" I yelled. "I did it!"

"You sure did," said Pa. I glanced at him. He was grinning so much his face nearly split in half.

Maybe I was a natural sportsman after all! I grinned back. I practiced all morning. I reeled the line in, then flicked it out, watching it sing across the river. If this was fishing, then I must be a fisherman. I loved it! It was fantastic, wonderful, awesome.

Pa stood in the water a little way from me, and every time I looked at him, he was still grinning. With a part of my mind, I knew I was cold, but I couldn't drag myself out of the water.

Then I got a bite. I'd forgotten that if you go fishing, you sometimes catch a fish.

Pa was over the moon. He stood beside me and talked that fish out of the water. "Steady," he whispered. "It'll try to run." Sure enough, the fish took off, the line screaming from the reel.

Then it stopped. "Reel it in," Pa said. "Steady as she goes."

I reeled it in, the rod bending as the fish pulled, then it took off again.

"My stars!" Pa whispered. "It's a monster! You've got the old man of the mountains for sure!" Excitement made his voice tremble, but he never took his eyes off the fish. He talked to it. "What a fighter! That's it, my beauty! Run for it!" And he talked to me. "Steady, Jimmy. Nice and easy. Keep it coming. That's right. You're doing great!"

I played that fish. Even without Pa there beside me, I reckon I'd have known what to do. It was like there was something sitting on my shoulder, making my hands work. I knew when to wind the line in, when to wait, and when to let it go. All the time, I watched the struggling fish. It was a contest, between it and me. Each of us were trying to outwit the other. It tried every trick in the river – it darted and turned and flashed through sunlight and shadow. It rested, then took off like a rocket. But all the time, my mind was one step ahead. Nothing that trout could do was going to beat me.

I guess I had to win. I was bigger and stronger, and it hadn't managed to get off the hook. I got it close to me. "A trout!" I breathed.

"What did you expect?" Pa asked. "A whale?" He reached for the net. "This is the tricky part. Don't let him get between your legs or we'll lose him." He slipped the net under the fish and lifted it into the air. "What a beauty!"

The trout's sides heaved and the rainbow colors shimmered in the sun. The fish flapped and twisted, almost as if it was trying to fly out of the net. I stood in the water and watched it. A frantic twist

turned it around so that I could see its eyes. They were wide and staring, and I could almost feel its panic. I had fought it for fun, but it had fought me for its life. I lifted it out of the net and squatted down in the water holding the fish with one hand while I twisted the hook out of its mouth with the other. Then I slid it back into the pool. It disappeared – forever, if it had any sense.

All at once, I felt cold again. I hugged my arms around my body, trying to stop the shivers. I stood up and slowly turned around to face Pa.

He loomed above me, huge in his dark waders. He gasped a few times, then he let loose with a huge, bellowing roar. "What did you do that for, you goof? That was the biggest fish I've seen in forty years and YOU THREW IT BACK!" He stood in the water, glaring at me. "Well? I'm waiting, boy! Why?" His eyebrows met across his nose and his face was bright red.

I couldn't stay in the water another second. I stumbled out and stood on the bank, trembling with cold and fright. He'd never understand. At last I said, "It fought so hard."

"Huh!" he exploded and stomped out of the water, making sure I got good and splashed as he went by. He scorched me with an enraged look, grabbed his sweatshirt from the bank, and stormed off. I heard him spit out the word, "Weak!"

I collapsed on the stubbly grass, rubbing my arms. Why had I come? He hated me. I was nothing like my father, and I never would be.

Chapter Four

I sat there for ages, watching the sky and watching the water. The noises of late summer buzzed in my ears, and it was as if I was alone in the world, but it wasn't my world.

When I'd warmed up again, I slid into the water and floated on the current down to our campsite. I was hungry and sad. I looked at all of the food Pa had brought and decided we'd have a can of beans for lunch. I ate a piece of dry bread while I waited for him.

He came striding down the river – without a fish. He just nodded when I said, "How about beans for lunch?"

I lit the burner and poured the beans into the pot. He didn't say anything until I dished out his half. "Why, Jimmy? Why did you just throw that fish away? It was such a beauty!"

I stared at him. It felt like there was a mile-high wall between us. Whatever I said, he'd never understand. I took a deep breath and tried to explain. "I just felt sorry for the fish. It was beautiful, and it has a right to live."

"It's a sport, Jimmy." He practically spat the words at me.

"Not for the fish," I said, spitting a bit myself.

"It's a fair fight... a test of skill." He spoke slowly as if he was explaining something difficult to a little kid – and maybe he was. "It's man against fish, and may the best one win."

I swallowed all the things I wanted to say, things like, "Pick on something your own size," and said nothing. He ate his beans and didn't speak to me again about it, but it was there, hovering between us like an unexploded bomb.

He didn't rinse his plate after lunch. "You can clean up," he snapped. "I'm going to go catch something for dinner."

I watched him pull on his waders. I guess if I'd turned out to be a natural sportsman, then he'd have given me waders for my birthday. My father's fishing rod lay in the grass beside me. I wondered if he would let me keep it. Did I even want to keep it?

I got up and put away the lunch stuff. There was still a day and a half left before we got to leave.

It was going to be pretty bad, with Pa snarling at me every time he caught sight of me. I sat on a rock that was hot from the sun, and wondered what I should do.

What I really wanted to do was explore up the river, but that was where Pa was, and he would not be impressed if he saw me.

But maybe he didn't need to see me. If I could sneak past him, then he wouldn't even need to know I was there, contaminating his river with my unsportsmanlike presence.

I rubbed on some more sunscreen, pulled my wet T-shirt back on, and headed up the river, moving as if I were stalking an enemy. He wasn't by the rapids that we'd crossed in the morning, and he'd given up on the pool where I'd caught my fish. I slid into the water and swam hard against the current until I got to the top of the pool where the river curved around a corner. I pushed my way against the current, stumbling and slipping until I could see up the next stretch of river. I crouched behind a rock and peered cautiously around it.

Pa was there, halfway along, striding to get to the next pool. He had his back to me, so I stood up and fought the speed of the water where it crashed down from the rapids until I was standing on the bank.

He half turned and I dropped to my knees, peering at him through the straggly bushes. Had he seen me? I didn't think so. He took a step forward, swinging his way through the water. If I'd been him, I'd have jumped from rock to rock – there were some big ones sticking out of the water. But he just kept walking and didn't even put a hand on the rocks to keep his balance.

The bank I was on butted into a cliff. The only way forward was by water. I slid into the river, my eyes on Pa. But he was nearly at the next pool, and I didn't think he'd turn around now. Just in case, I stayed low in the water and scrambled from rock to rock so I could duck down to hide if he did turn around.

I was enjoying stalking him. I thought that maybe I was a natural sportsman after all – a natural at grandfather stalking. My eyes skimmed the river ahead of me. I'd head for the lumpy rock out in mid-stream, about ten feet ahead. I glanced up to see where Pa was. I blinked at what I saw – or rather, didn't see. The river was empty. Then I saw a splash from behind the biggest rock in the rapids. "Ha!" I yelled, standing up. "You're not going to catch me twice with that trick! Get up, Pa! I know you're not drowning!"

I felt a little better. He must've forgiven me if he was up to playing tricks again. Then I saw something else, and it froze my blood. His fishing net was drifting down the river toward me, being tumbled over and over in the current. He'd never let it go, and if he dropped it by accident, he'd be making a huge noise about getting it back – which he wasn't.

"Pa!" I screamed. I hurled myself into the water. The net hit a rock then spun toward me. I launched myself toward it in a belly flop and just managed to catch hold of the handle. I held onto the net part and used the handle to propel myself through the force of the rushing water. "Pa!" I yelled again, but there was no movement from behind the rock. I'd let him have it if he was tricking me. No, I'd be so glad, I'd sit down and bawl my eyes out, and that'd *really* teach him.

It seemed to take forever to reach the rock that hid him, but looking back, it couldn't have been more than a few seconds. Every step I took I yelled, "Pa!" But it made no difference. There was no sign of him. I stumbled through the water, using the net to keep my balance. It helped, but I was moving so slowly. I imagined Pa lying under the water, not being able to breathe, and my own breath choked in my chest.

I kept my eyes on the rock. I couldn't see him in the water. Had the current washed him downstream? Could that have happened and I hadn't seen? I gasped, choking for air. I was at the rock, and I fell on it, trying to breathe, trying to look down through the churning water.

He was there. I could see him under the water, not moving, and the water had filled up his waders so that he was fat like a balloon man. Suddenly I could breathe easier. I clawed my way around to where he was lying. He was totally submerged, and his body was pushed up against the rock by the current. "Pa!" I shrieked again, uselessly. I shoved myself upstream of him, ducked under, and grabbed his shoulders. I heaved and tugged at his head and shoulders. He moved slightly, and I shoved his head above the water, but I couldn't lift him high enough to get him out. My lungs were bursting. I broke through to the surface, gulped some air, and tried again. The water poured over him, pushing him down again.

"Pa, get up!" I screamed, straining every muscle to try to lift him. He was going to die, and I couldn't do anything to help him. I tried to lift him again. A gulp of air, under the water, pull, heave, tug. Nothing worked, not even when I got the straps of his waders undone. I stood up, swiping the water from my face, and hoping that miraculously somebody would be there on the bank who could help me. There was nobody. I looked down at him and I couldn't see, because tears were pouring from my eyes. He was back under the water, and I couldn't do a thing about it. He was going to die.

Something hardened in my mind. I had maybe a minute before it was too late. I had to think. I couldn't keep doing the same thing again. Do something different. Think. I scrubbed at my eyes and tried to take slow breaths. I couldn't pull him out of the water, but could I push him?

It was all I could try, there was no time to do anything else. I took a huge breath and ducked under the water. I wriggled and pushed until my head and shoulders were underneath his chest, and then I started straightening my legs. My lungs were bursting. Would I die, too? Suddenly he shifted. The current was helping now, lifting him to the top. My head popped out into the air, and I gulped, sucking air into my chest. I kept pushing and finally got most of him up on the flat rock he'd washed up against. I wrapped my arms around him to keep him from sliding back into the current.

He wasn't breathing. Keep calm. If you panic, he'll die.

I dropped down beside him and yanked him the rest of the way out of the water until he was lying flat on his back on the rock. Two years ago, when I'd been a Boy Scout, a lady had come in to teach us CPR. I shut my eyes for a moment and remembered the words. Listen, look, feel. I put my ear next to his mouth. I couldn't hear any sign of breathing or see that his chest was moving at all.

Okay, the first thing I needed to do was to get some air into him. I tilted his head back gently, pinched his nose shut, and breathed into his mouth two times – was that the right number? I paused and did the same thing about five seconds later and continued this pattern for about a minute. The next thing I had to do was see if his heart was beating. I felt for a pulse on the side of his neck, and although it took my half-frozen fingers a few seconds to feel it, there was definitely something there. His heart was still beating!

But now what... should I keep doing what I had just done? Had he been under the water too long? I pushed the questions away and kept repeating the drill. I could almost hear the other scouts counting along. One, two, pause... one, two, pause. Pa, don't die. There was a gash on his head, and blood started oozing out of it. Did that mean he was alive? Hadn't I seen something on television that said that a if a person is dead then he doesn't bleed?

Come on, Pa, start breathing! I don't know how long I stayed there, trying to breathe for him. It felt like forever, but suddenly he coughed. I pulled back. Water was filling his mouth, choking him. I rolled him onto his side, and it gushed out of his mouth. Was he breathing on his own? He coughed again, and then he spluttered a bit, but it looked like he was breathing again!

"Oh, Pa!" I whispered, rolling him gently back. I looked again at the blood that was oozing out of the wound on his head. "Pa, can you hear me? Your head's bleeding. Can you hear me?" I repeated desperately.

He grunted and put his hand to his head as if he wasn't quite sure what had happened. He struggled to raise himself but couldn't, even with me trying to support his shoulders. He collapsed back onto the rock.

"Where's my fishing rod?" he muttered. "Jimmy, if you've lost my rod…"

His rod? He was worrying about his rod? "Pa, are you okay? You cut your head." I took off my shirt. "You're bleeding all over the place. We'll have bears and mountain lions after us any minute now. Let me tie this around your head." I spoke slowly, trying to sound calm and confident, but what I really wanted to do was put my head down and bawl my eyes out like a little kid. I wanted him to put his arm around me and say, "You did a good job, kiddo!" My hands shook as I tried to tie my shirt around his head.

He swiped at my hand. "Stop bothering me, boy. Go and get your grandmother. She'll fix me up. I'm just a little dizzy, that's all."

I gulped. Grandma? Didn't he even know where we were? Didn't he know that I'd just hauled him out of a river and that he'd nearly drowned? Suddenly I was aware of how cold I was. I began to wrap my soaking shirt around his head again. "Pa, your head's bleeding a lot. I have to take care of you." I hoped he'd feel better when the blood wasn't pouring out of him. My hands shook. Somebody help me – I can't do this by myself. "Pa, can you walk? Let's get back to the tent."

Instead of answering, he just shook his head as if there was something inside it that was loose. He tried to heave himself up again, then he sank back with a groan. "It seems I've hurt my leg, Jimmy."

I slid off the rock and stood beside him, my hands feeling gently down his right leg, but I couldn't tell anything through the waders. "We'll have to get these off you, Pa," I said. He didn't seem to hear me, but just lay there with his eyes shut. "Pa!" I yelled and I shook his left leg. "You have to take the waders off!"

He opened his eyes and glared at me. "Don't be crazy, boy. You know that I can't walk on the stones without waders."

I shut my eyes, trying to will away my panic. He wasn't thinking straight. What was I going to do? Here we were, in the middle of a river, in the middle of nowhere – a skinny weak kid and an old man who'd had the sense knocked out of him and was badly hurt to boot.

Chapter Five

I fought back the panic that was trying to take over my mind.

"Pa," I said slowly and clearly. "Sit up straight. I need to get the waders off of you. I need to see your leg."

I waited, shivering and hoping. But slowly, he pushed himself upright, lurched onto his left leg, and held himself up off the rock with his hands. I tugged at the waders and got them down around his legs before he collapsed onto the rock again.

"My leg hurts," he muttered. "I must've done something to it."

I crouched in the water, fighting to free his legs from the waders. He groaned a bit when I touched his right leg. "Just get on with it," he grunted when I stopped. At last, it was done. There was a huge bump in the bone that went from his ankle to his knee. I was almost sure it was broken.

I stood up, tipped the water out of the waders, and said slowly, "Pa, can you hear me?"

"I'm not deaf," he grumbled, "just a little dizzy. Go get your mother, Graham."

I swallowed, and my heart was thumping. Graham was my-father's name. He thought I was my father. "Sure, Pa." I fought to keep my voice steady. "You just sit here and don't move while I get her. Okay?"

"Just go, lad. I don't feel so good." He sat slumped with his head in his hands.

I stumbled through the water to the bank, clasping the waders in my arms. Don't faint and roll in again, Pa.

I had to get him out of the river and onto the beach first. I wanted to go back to the camp and get the little hatchet so I could cut a stick for him to lean on, but I didn't dare leave him. I searched the river bank, all the time watching him, but he didn't move. There was driftwood farther up the bank, tangled in tree roots. I made myself stop and look for the best way to climb up. Then I forced myself to go slowly and carefully. I could see a branch that looked just like what I needed. It wasn't too long, and it had a strong fork at one end. I hung onto a tree root with one hand and pulled at the branch with the other. Once, when I glanced at Pa, I saw him move. He tried to sit up, but he slumped back again. He'd roll off the rock for sure if I didn't hurry. I heaved at the branch. Seconds later it clattered onto the rocks below.

I slid down the bank and grabbed it. He was still on the rock, just sitting there, shaking his head every now and then and shivering. "It's okay, Pa!" I called, "I'm coming." But I don't think he heard.

I'd gone in upstream of him, so it was easy to use the current to get back to him. I didn't know if it would be better to let the current help get Pa to the bank, or if it would be better to take the shortest way we could. In the end, I looked for the best landing place and decided that we should head for that.

I thought we'd never get there. He swayed when I hauled him to his feet, and his face was gray. I kept shouting at him, hoping I could get through to him.

"Pa, lean on the stick, that's right, now lean on me and hop forward. That's it! Good job!" He was so heavy, he nearly pushed me down into the rocks, and I could tell that his leg was hurting like crazy. He didn't say anything, though; he just kept his mouth shut tight and did everything I told him. Once, he stumbled when a stone turned under his foot. He fell forward, and all his weight punched down on my shoulder. I went down like I'd been hit, and my head went right under the water. But somehow he managed to shove himself upright again. I came up choking.

"Sorry, Jimmy lad," he muttered. At least I was Jimmy again and not my father.

We inched our way across the river. Every stone hurt him. It hurt the foot he was walking on and the jarring and hopping hurt the leg he had broken. He didn't say a word, but sometimes he gave a small grunt.

Just when I thought his face couldn't get any more gray, or the lines on his forehead any deeper, we reached the bank. He collapsed onto the grass and lay there with his eyes shut. Carefully, I lifted his legs out of the water. Even though it must have hurt him, he didn't even groan. But he was so close to the edge of the river. "Pa, can you pull yourself forward a little?" I asked softly. I was shaking and it wasn't just because I was cold.

He didn't say anything or open his eyes. Instead he just turned onto his stomach with immense effort and dragged himself maybe a yard from the water. He lay there, looking like a beached whale that has come to land to die. I had thought that getting him to dry land would make everything okay, but it didn't. I was frightened that he still might die.

I was so tired and cold, and all I wanted was for him to get up and make everything all right. But he couldn't. It was up to me. I was the one who had to make it all right again – if I could.

I put my hand on his forehead. His skin was clammy and cold. I stared around. He needed to be warm, but all of our supplies were down at the camp. Except the waders. I stood up on shaky legs and staggered over to where I'd dumped them when I'd hunted for the stick. The outside of them was already dry and quite warm to the touch. He could lie on them, and if I could get his wet clothes off, then he might warm up in the sun while I went down to the camp for some gear.

"Pa? Listen, I'm going to help you get your wet clothes off. Okay?"

He didn't say anything. I didn't know if he even heard me. Getting his sweatshirt off wasn't so bad. I pulled his arms through the sleeves and then pulled it off over his head. He didn't move while I was doing it, except to shiver. The shirt was more difficult. Even though it buttoned down the front, it didn't stretch like the sweatshirt did, and I had to roll him from side to side to pull it off. His eyelids fluttered. "I feel sick."

I sat back in horror. What if he was sick, and what if he choked? I rolled him onto his side again, like I had back on the rock when he was choking on the water. Once I had him in place, I bent his left leg at the knee to keep him from rolling onto his back again.

I sat back on my heels to assess the situation and felt another sinking feeling. How dumb! I was just so dumb. Why hadn't I pulled his trousers off first? Now I had to move him all over again.

There was no use waiting around, hoping they'd slide off all by themselves. I got up. "Sorry, Pa," I whispered. "Sorry." The buttonhole on the waistband was wet and stiff. It took maybe half a minute before I got it undone. Then I had to get the heavy soaking trousers off him. If only I could have grabbed onto the bottoms of the legs and pulled, it would have been easy, but I didn't dare do that because of hurting his leg.

Still, I had to try something. Bit by bit, I pushed the trousers down, then I wriggled and shoved and tugged until I got them clear of his hips. He moaned once, and I heard him mutter, "Graham, get your mother." But at last it was done. He lay on the grass, and his skin was pale and felt sort of cold and damp. I could see the bump in his right leg clearly. It should be tied up and supported somehow – a splint. I should tie a splint over it. Now? Or later, after I got the stuff from the camp up here?

I rubbed my head, trying to think, trying to make up my mind about what was the best thing to do. Later, I decided. There wasn't much point in fixing his leg if he froze to death.

I looked at the waders. He'd be more comfortable lying on them rather than on the dry spiky grass – but it would also mean I'd have to move him again. I decided to leave him where he was for now.

I bent over him, my hand on his shoulder. "Pa, I have to go down to the campsite and get some gear. I'll be as quick as I can."

He grunted. I tried to tie the T-shirt around his head again, but he brushed me away.

"Leave me alone, boy. Get your grandmother."

Apparently, sometimes he knew who I was, and sometimes he didn't. I didn't want to leave him in this state. I sat beside him for a moment, trying to think about what I needed from the camp. There were so many things, I'd have to make several trips because there was no way I'd ever be able to carry all of it at once. Unless... My hand fell on the waders. Maybe I could put some of the gear in them and pull them through the water behind me.

The idea gave me enough energy to get up. All I could do was try.

Getting back to the camp was easy. I just fell into the water and floated down the rapids and through the two deep pools until I got there.

The first thing I thought of was food. With a shock, I realized I was starving. How could I worry about being hungry when Pa was lying there, wet and cold and maybe dying?

My stomach growled. "All right!" I muttered. My chocolate bars. I poured out the contents of my pack. Pa had said they'd melt, and he'd been right, but I ate one anyway. Then I had three cookies. "Enough," I told myself. "Now get to work." But I felt stronger to face what lie ahead.

Maybe Pa needed food. Or maybe that's just what he shouldn't have. I wished I knew.

In my head, I heard Mom's voice repeating what she often told me, "Just think carefully, and do the best you can."

What I had to do right now was pack some gear. I decided to take my pack. Pa's was just too big. It might overbalance me, and I didn't want to dump our supplies into the river.

I filled my pack with Pa's dry clothes, some for me, some food, the gas burner, and Pa's sleeping bag. Then I got my sleeping bag, air mattress, and the groundsheet and stuffed them inside one leg of the waders. I put the tent down the other leg. I left behind Pa's pack, our hiking boots, and my father's fishing rod.

I picked up the hatchet. A stick would be handy. I would need it to keep myself from slipping as I went back up the river. It didn't take long to find one and chop it to the right length. I jammed the hatchet into the waders, then I picked up the pack and hefted it onto my back.

With the stick in one hand, and pulling the waders with the other, I walked to the edge of the water.

As soon as I got there, I saw that it wasn't going to work. I wasn't going to be able to hold the waders up high enough to keep the water from pouring in. I struggled to pull the waders through the bushes along the edge of the river while I thought about the problem. Maybe I could carry the waders, holding them tight against my chest, but I'd really need two hands to do that. That would make it almost impossible to walk against the current in the deeper pools. No, I was going to need to keep my hands free for balance.

I gave up on that idea. I still hadn't figured out what I was going to do when I got to the place where the grass edge got too steep to walk on. I let go of the waders. I'd just have to make two trips. I was actually in the water when the idea hit me. I scrambled out and grabbed the waders. Quickly, I took my pack off, fastened the straps of the waders around the straps of my pack, and put it on again. When I got in the water, the waders floated behind me, but they were pulled up high enough to prevent any water from pouring in.

I plunged through the river with a fat grin on my face. It was weird, but I felt as if I'd conquered a mountain.

Chapter Six

I had to cross several tricky areas to get back to Pa. Luckily, the river bank beside both of the deep pools was flat enough to walk on or I would have sunk so deep that our supplies would have gotten soaked, and then I would have been in real trouble.

I got to the rapids where Pa had fallen. I glanced up and saw the rock, but I didn't look at it again – instead, I just focused on walking across the current. It was tricky because the waders dragged at me. I was glad I had the stick. I stumbled several times and would have fallen if I hadn't had it.

Pa was exactly as I'd left him, and for a moment, I thought he was dead.

"Pa?" I was too frightened to do more than whisper. "Pa? Are you okay?" I could have reached out and touched him, but I didn't. Instead, I sat on the grass, shrugged my shoulders out of the pack, and tugged at the waders to pull them up beside me. I couldn't bear to look at Pa.

For almost a minute, I sat where I was, half turned away from him. But I knew I had to move. I had to do something. Slowly, I stretched my hand toward him. "Pa?"

He was so still. My hand hovered above his shoulder. I took a breath that was more like a sob and let my hand drop onto his skin. It felt exactly like it had when I'd left him – sort of clammy and cold, even though there was a faint redness where the sun was starting to burn it. I still wasn't sure whether he was dead or alive. I knelt beside him and bent to press my ear to his chest. I heard the thud of his heart beat.

I sat up, tears welling up in my eyes again. He was alive. He was still alive.

Hastily, I swiped the back of my hand across my eyes. This was no time to act like a baby. I still had so much to do. First, I shook out Pa's sleeping bag, unzipped it, and lay it over him. The next thing to do, I decided, was to put a splint on his leg. Getting the sticks was easy enough. I used the hatchet and got some dry driftwood that was strong but not too thick. The real problem came when I looked around for something to tie them on with.

All I had was the dry clothes I'd brought for each of us, and the wet ones I'd taken off Pa. I couldn't use the dry clothes and the wet ones would make him cold.

While I thought about it, I undid my air mattress and blew it up. At this point, I didn't care whether he thought I was weak. I was going to get Pa onto that air mattress if I could possibly manage it. I set it aside – ready for when I'd need it.

Next, I decided to dry our wet clothes. The shadows were long by now, and the day was dying. "There's only one thing for me to do, Pa," I said. Somehow, it was comforting to talk to him, even though he didn't answer. "I'll have to build a fire."

He'd have yelled at me about that, for sure. A natural hunter would never light a fire in a place that was as dry as old paper. Too bad. Anyway, a fire would cheer me up. But I filled up the cooking pot with water, just in case.

It was easy to collect enough wood. I chose a place near the water – just in case things went wrong. There was a hollow that had rocks around it. I got the hatchet and scraped most of the grass away. Then I piled up a heap of little twigs and sticks. Before I lit it, I heaped bigger branches close by and I spread the wet clothes on the rocks.

The flame sparked out of Pa's lighter and jumped into the twigs. They didn't burn, but the grass did. Even though I'd gotten rid of most of it, I watched, fascinated, as a dry root lying on the ground shriveled and glowed. The next thing I knew, there was a burning patch at my feet and it was spreading fast. Unbelievable – somehow I'd managed to start a grass fire! I grabbed Pa's

trousers and flung them on top of the crackling grass. Flames escaped from the edges. I snatched his soaking sweatshirt and bashed at the flames, and even kicked dirt at them with my bare feet. I dumped the pot of water on them. I looked around wildly. Flames were licking up beside the trousers. I threw the sweatshirt on top of them, dived for the pot, dunked it in the water, and threw load after load of water at the fire.

By the time I was sure it was out, I was exhausted, dirty, and had sore feet – but worst of all, I felt so stupid. Pa would kill me when he found out.

And on top of everything else, I still hadn't thought of what I could use to splint his leg.

The sun was sinking lower. I got my dry T-shirt and sweatshirt out of my pack and put them on. Should I use those? I shook my head. I couldn't decide. I tucked the sleeping bag more firmly around Pa. He still looked awful, and he still felt cold. I would have to do something – he'd get very cold lying on the bare ground all night. But I didn't want to move him again – even to get him on the air mattress – without splinting his leg first.

"Pa! What should I do? It's too hard. I can't do this by myself!"

I stood up. Stupid! This was so stupid. If I started thinking like that, I might as well lie down beside Pa and we could both die.

I was the only one who could save him. So I'd better get on with it. But how? I thought about it. I don't mean an idea sort of buzzed into my head and I grabbed it and said, yeah, that's it. I mean I *really* thought about it. First: should I use my dry clothes to tie on the splints? I decided that unless I really couldn't think of anything else, I wouldn't, because if I had to walk around during the night to look after Pa, then I'd get really cold if I didn't have any dry clothes to wear.

I looked at the other things I had, and I spent a while getting really annoyed that Pa had chucked out stuff like my extra T-shirts and towel. Before I knew it, I was so ticked off at him that I actually wanted to scream at him for getting me into this situation.

That scared me – really scared me. Here was Pa, helpless and unconscious and maybe almost dead. And me? Instead of doing something to help

64

him, I was wasting precious time thinking he was a jerk. Why did he always bring out the worst in me? Maybe my father would have had the exact same effect on me. But that was something I was never going to know.

I tucked my hands under my arms and tried to think more constructively.

What if I used my sleeping bag? I could cut long strips out of it with Pa's fishing knife. Really, while the idea made sense, it was the last thing I wanted to do. I was so tired and it was starting to get cold. It was so tempting to crawl into the bag and lie down on my air mattress.

"Aw, the heck with it," I said, standing up. Pa's knife was on the ground beside him. I picked it up and started hacking away at the sleeping bag. It turned out to be a good choice because it had padding that I wrapped around Pa's leg before I tied on the sticks.

It was harder than I'd thought it would be. Another pair of hands would have helped a lot, and I wished I was an octopus.

At last it was done, and I have to say I was pretty proud of my work.

"Hey, Pa! What do you think? Cool, huh?" I kept on talking to him. He kept on not answering. Still, it filled up the silence and drowned out the thoughts in my head.

Getting him onto the air mattress was tough, too, because he was so big and heavy. I rolled him, first onto his side, bit by bit, and then onto his front. I slid the mattress under him as I rolled him back over. Once that task was done, I noticed that his skin still felt cold and clammy. I put his dry sweatshirt over his head, got one arm in, and pulled it down as far as I could. Then I wrapped his flannel shirt around his waist like a skirt. I used his dry trousers to support his bad leg and then tucked the sleeping bag around him.

He didn't say a word the whole time. He didn't even groan. I dragged the tent over and managed to rig up a sort of shelter. It wasn't great, but it'd keep the dew off us. I was hungry, but I was too tired to do anything about it. Instead, I crawled in beside Pa, wrapped the scrap of my sleeping bag that was left around me, and huddled close to him.

Pa, don't die.

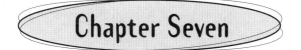

Chapter Seven

His muttering woke me up when it was totally dark. "Pa? Are you okay?" I put my hand on his shoulder.

He wriggled as if to shake it off. "Cut it out, Graham! When are you going to grow up? You do the dumbest things!"

I snatched my hand back, my mind spinning. Did my father used to get on his nerves, like I always seem to do?

Cautiously, I sat up and tucked the sleeping bag more snugly around him. I couldn't see what I was doing. If only I had a flashlight, but if he'd packed one, I hadn't seen it anywhere. I leaned over him and put my hand on his forehead. He was feeling a bit warmer.

I lay down again, my stomach rumbling. Even so, I quickly fell back to sleep.

It was almost daylight when I woke up again. Pa was stirring, then he groaned, choking the sound off quickly.

"Pa? Pa, is there anything I can do to help you?" I sat up, my head hitting the sagging roof of the tent.

He didn't answer, and when I leaned over to peer at him I saw that he had his mouth shut tight, fighting pain.

I wriggled out of the tent. Maybe a cup of coffee would help him. And what about something warm to eat? If only I knew what to do – what was best for him.

Outside, the morning was gray and silent, except for the shivering sounds of the river. I filled the pot and lit the burner. While it was heating, I searched through the food. More rice. Too much trouble. There was a can of stew. I decided on that. I made enough coffee for each of us to have a cup. Normally, I thought coffee was revolting, but I was wanting something warm to drink in the chilly morning. When the coffee was ready, I poured the can of stew into the pot.

I wriggled back under the tent. "Pa? I made coffee. Do you want some?"

I was holding my breath. Pa always wanted coffee. Even if he'd already drunk the tank dry, he would always have another cup. The way I saw it, if he didn't want coffee, then he was in even worse shape than I'd thought.

He muttered something I couldn't hear. I crawled in until I was beside him. I put the mug into his hand. He managed to get it to his mouth and gulped at it. "Good. That's good," he muttered. "Do you have any more, Graham?"

I wanted to scream, "I'm Jim, I'm not my father!" But what was the use? I wriggled back out of the tent and got my own mug of coffee, stirred the stew, and went back to Pa.

He gulped at the second mugful, then grunted in a sort of whisper, "Get your mother, Graham. Why do I have to tell you things so many times?"

I took the mug, my hand shaking. Somehow, I'd thought the coffee would be magic, that it would clear his mind and he'd sit up and tell me what to do. "Would you like something to eat, Pa?"

He grunted. It might have meant yes. I went and got the stew. The smell of it had me drooling. I grabbed a spoonful or two as I struggled back to Pa. It just made me hungrier than ever.

I knelt beside him. "Pa, here's some stew. Are you hungry?"

His lips moved. "I could eat a whale, Graham."

I blinked hard and held the spoon to his lips. He ate about half of what I'd put in the bowl, then he turned his head slightly and shut his mouth. His eyes were closed. For a second, I wondered if he'd died, but then he whispered, "Thanks, son."

I sat up, shaking. Who did he think was helping him – me or my father?

There was no way I'd go back to sleep now. I tucked the sleeping bag around him as well as I could and then sat outside. The air was chilly. I ate the rest of the stew, but I was still hungry. I took out another of my mangled chocolate bars. Luckily, the melting hadn't changed its taste.

Then an awful thought crashed into my head. I should be saving food.

We were supposed to hike back out tomorrow and Grandma was supposed to pick us up at five o'clock. She'd probably wait for an hour or so until she was sure we weren't coming. Then it would be the next day before a search party would start looking for us – and they might find us quickly, or they might not.

Well, I could always catch a fish.

Pa groaned. I stuck my head in the tent, but he seemed to be asleep. I sat down again and watched the light grow stronger as the sun came up.

All sorts of ideas raced through my head, but the main one was that we had to get help today. Pa wasn't doing too well – even a twelve-year-old kid with no medical training could tell that. He was pale and, although he wasn't cold and clammy anymore, he was out cold most of the time. When he was awake, he didn't even know who I was.

He kept calling me Graham, but he was growling at me as if I was me. I turned my head to stare at the tent. Had my father been an ordinary kid, too? At that moment, I decided I would like to take the fishing rod home with me. It'd be kind of nice to have something of my father's.

I stood up and stamped my feet, trying to warm up a little. Those sort of thoughts could wait. Right now, I needed to concentrate on the important stuff.

I was tempted to light a signal fire, although I knew it could set the whole place alight. The only thing that stopped me was that even though I'd been able to rescue Pa from the river, I knew I'd have no chance of hauling him out of a forest fire.

I divided up the food into three piles, one for today, the second for the day we had planned to hike out, and the third for the day of waiting to be rescued. It didn't seem like nearly enough. I would just have to figure out a way to get help today. In the back of my mind was the constant worry that if Pa didn't get some medical attention, he might die.

A signal would be good. I tugged my tattered sleeping bag out and climbed up the hill with it. I flung it over a bush so that it stretched out, bright red among the green and brown of the forest.

But a signal only works if somebody sees it – and understands it. What if the helicopter that we saw the first day noticed it but thought it was just there to dry or something? I couldn't let myself start thinking like that. The only thing that kept that awful, hopeless feeling away was keeping busy.

I slithered back down the hill and looked in at Pa. His eyes flickered. "Coffee," he whispered.

That gave me something to do. I boiled some more water and tried to come up with a signal to get us some help. Pa lifted his head slightly to gulp at his coffee. "Good," he muttered. "That's good."

"Are you hungry, Pa?" I asked.

"No, Graham, but my leg hurts." His eyes drifted closed again and I backed out of the tent.

I started collecting a pile of sticks. It wasn't to burn them. Yesterday's little adventure was sharp in my mind. It just gave me something to do. And it made me hungry. Pa was asleep, so I decided to have a can of spaghetti. I ate it cold because I didn't know how long the gas in the canister would last and I didn't want to explain to Pa that I couldn't make him some coffee when he wanted it.

Cold spaghetti isn't the world's greatest meal, but it filled me up. Mom would laugh when I told her. I could be pretty picky about my food sometimes, and there was no way that I'd ever eat cold spaghetti at home. It was dangerous to think about Mom. It raised a big lump in my throat. I got up and threw some more wood around.

Sometime later, I heard Pa groan. I jumped up and stuck my head inside the tent. "Pa? What can I get you?"

"I've got to go to the bathroom, boy. Help me up, will you?"

Oh great! "Hang on, Pa – I'll get you something. You better stay where you are."

He stopped trying to heave himself up. "It hurts a bit, boy. But be quick, will you?"

I backed out of the tent and stared at the gear. The cooking pot. Would that work? I picked it up, but it was pretty small – and I have to say that I didn't like the idea of eating stuff that had been cooked in a pot that had doubled as a latrine.

Pa sort of groaned again. "It's okay, Pa. This is just going to take a sec!"

What could I use? There was nothing except the pot. I even wondered about using my pack – but it would leak. Then my eyes fell on the waders. I gave a yell of triumph. Just what I needed. I grabbed Pa's fishing knife and hacked until I had chopped one boot away from the top part.

I took it to Pa. "Here, Pa – try to use this."

Luckily, he didn't ask what it was, because I kind of guessed he wouldn't be impressed at the sight of a chopped-up wader. Anyway, it did the job. And it was lucky I hadn't tried to use the cooking pot. I took the boot, emptied it into the river, and washed it out.

It was about then that I had my brilliant idea.

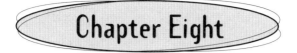

Chapter Eight

I could burn the boots.

They were rubber and I happened to know that burning rubber makes very black smoke. In science class last year, our teacher did an experiment to show why burning tires can cause such awful pollution. She took us all outside and even though she just burned up a small rubber ball, the thick black smoke that it raised was impressive.

I stood there, holding the boot and frowning at it. If I burned it, it would still be a fire and it could still get away from me and burn the whole camp – including Pa. I stared around me. If I took it into the middle of the river and set fire to it on a rock it should be pretty safe.

I checked on Pa. He seemed to be asleep, although he was muttering a little bit, and every now and then he'd start groaning. His face was gray. I pulled my head out of the tent. I would burn the boots and take my chances. Pa had to have help, and quickly.

Mom's words swam back into my head: "Just think carefully and do the best you can." Think carefully. What else was there to think about? Fire? I'd thought about that, and being in the middle of the river should take care of it.

So, Jim, what is the fire for, I asked myself.

It's a signal, beetle brain.

And how long is that signal going to last, Jim?

That made me stop. I had a boot and a long stick in one hand and the gas burner and lighter in the other. I was already wading out into the river, but at that thought, I turned back to the bank and sat down on the sand again. Even if a fire watcher saw my smoke signal, it'd take a helicopter longer to get here than the smoke would last. Would they keep looking, or would they stop worrying if there was no more smoke? They wouldn't know it was a distress signal. Nobody was even expecting us to come out until tomorrow.

I needed some other signal. I stared up at the ridge. The red of the sleeping bag looked like a bright gash on the ridge. It showed up well, but it still looked like a sleeping bag that had been stretched out to be aired.

I could cut it up. I'd have to make the pieces big enough so that they could be seen from as far away as possible. SOS? Would that work? I shook my head. It'd be too difficult to make the letters with a knife, and there was nowhere flat to lay them out.

In the end, I decided to cut the bag into three triangles and space them down the ridge, pointing to the camp. Pa seemed to be asleep – or unconscious – it was hard to tell, but he didn't respond when I told him what I was doing. I wished he'd yell at me, tell me not to be a weakling, or make me watch a hundred baseball games. But he just lay there, his face gray and his breathing shallow.

The sun was hot as I climbed the ridge. I sat in the shade to work on the sleeping bag. Pa's knife was as sharp as his tongue could be, but even so, I wasn't going to win any prizes in a straight-cutting competition. At last it was done. I put one of the triangles back where the sleeping bag had been.

I was standing on the ridge we'd walked in on, but above that there was another one, high and steep. It would be great to have a signal up there. I started climbing. It was too steep to get to the top. About halfway up there was a bare rock face. I

aimed for that. It was as high as I'd be able to get, and the rock would make the red stand out.

Climbing up through the bushes was tiring, but not difficult. The trees stopped at the rock face. I stared up – and up. It didn't look so easy anymore. How did you climb up a rock?

I pushed through the ferns and trees, looking for a place to climb up. In the end, I climbed on a dead tree trunk, scrambled from there to a little ledge on the rock, and found enough hand and toe holds to get up about twenty feet. I'd have liked to go higher – climbing that rock face felt terrific. Maybe I do have a little bit of my father in me after all. But I knew I was high enough for the signal to be visible, and that it'd be slightly inconvenient if I fell and hurt myself so badly that I couldn't move.

I jammed the two top corners of the red triangle into cracks in the rock and climbed back down. Carefully.

I set up the other triangle on the top of a rock halfway between the first one and the camp.

Back at the camp, Pa hadn't moved. Up on the ridges, the signals showed brightly against their backgrounds. I hoped the whole thing would work.

The latrine boot was still wet inside, so I hacked off the other boot as close to the nylon webbing as I could cut. I carefully put the gas burner and the lighter into it, picked up the long stick, and waded into the river. There was a big rock just about in the middle, and I headed for that.

I climbed up out of the water, set the burner on a fairly flat part, and lit it. I held the boot upside down over the flame. For a while, I thought it wasn't going to burn, but suddenly the flame caught and licked up the boot so fast that I nearly dropped it. I turned it the right way up and put it on the rock while I turned off the gas. The flames died down. I grabbed it and turned it upside down again. In seconds, the flames were leaping up the boot toward my hands.

There was plenty of thick black smoke rising into the still air, but I wasn't going to be able to hold the boot much longer. Idea! I grabbed the stick and shoved it into the boot. I held it away from me and waved it in circles, the black smoke drawing patterns in the clear air.

I was so pleased with the burning and with the smoke that I forgot why I was doing it. The boot

burned fiercely right until the end, and then it died, leaving me holding a glowing stick. Slowly, I lowered the stick into the water and watched the glow sizzle to death.

I sat on the rock and listened for the beat of a helicopter. I stayed there for ages, listening and waiting. Nothing happened.

I slid into the water. There was one more boot. I would burn the other boot. If nobody came this time, I would have big problems.

Because it was still a little wet, I thought it would take the second boot a long time to catch on fire, but it didn't seem to make any difference. I stood on the rock and held it on the stick. I didn't wave it around this time. Maybe it would last longer if I held it still. The smoke was black – but was there enough of it for somebody to see?

It seemed as if the second boot burned really quickly – even more quickly than the other one had. Too soon, I was standing on the rock with nothing more than a glowing stick that made hardly any smoke.

Around me I could hear the sounds of the river, crickets, and birds. But there were absolutely no machine-made sounds at all.

I got down from the rock and waded back to the bank. That was it. I had tried but it hadn't worked.

I sat down beside the tent and tried to think about what to do next.

I'd been sitting with my head in my hands for long enough to feel my arms burning when I heard it. I lifted my head, not daring to believe it was true – but you can't mistake the thumping noise a helicopter makes. I jumped up, tripped over, grabbed Pa's bright yellow shirt, ripped off my own blue T-shirt, and ran around, waving and yelling even though I couldn't see the helicopter, even though it still must have been a long way away.

Then I stopped. The noise was going away. It couldn't! It just couldn't be so cruel! I stood, straining my ears, trying to work out where it was. After about half a minute, I saw it – like a tiny dragonfly against the blue sky.

"Over here!" I bellowed, jumping around. They didn't have a hope of seeing me, but I kept jumping and waving. Suddenly, it seemed to turn and swoop down the valley. If it kept coming... if it followed the river... then they would see my signals. Wouldn't they?

Chapter Nine

I watched, holding my breath, fearing that any second it would veer away and disappear forever. But it kept coming, getting bigger and noisier. I started jumping again and waving. It was heading for the high signal on the cliff. It hovered in close, and the red triangle blew away in the wind, then it turned and followed the path of the other triangles. I jumped and danced and waved.

They saw me. A man leaned out and waved. I pointed at the tent. Would they understand? They hovered off to one side.

"Help!" I screamed, the word drowned by the chopper noise. I grabbed one of the tent ropes and yanked on it, dragging the tent back. "It's my grandfather!" I yelled. "He's hurt!"

I stared up, desperate for a way to make them understand.

The man leaned out of the door. He pointed to himself, then pointed away. He was yelling, too, but I couldn't figure out what he was saying.

Then the helicopter rose up and whirled away.

I sat down, shaking. Were they coming back? Would they tell somebody?

Of course they would.

I heard Pa mutter. "It's okay, Pa," I said. "That was a helicopter. They found us. We'll be home soon." If I said it enough times, would it come true? I pulled the tent back into place to keep the sun off him and sat down to wait.

It was the longest wait. I made Pa some more coffee. I cooked the rice because I was hungry and because I had to concentrate on how to do it.

I gave some to Pa, but he didn't want much. That really worried me. He never missed a meal normally. I ate mine slowly, making the time stretch out. I didn't want to be sitting there with nothing to do.

It was a long time before I heard something. I strained my ears, but after a few seconds I was sure. It was a helicopter.

I stood up on very wobbly legs. This time, I waited until I could see it before I went into my dance routine. It didn't fly directly over us the way the first one did. Instead, it hovered above the ridge. Then a man on a rope was lowered down on a harness.

I have to say he wasn't who I'd been expecting. I'd been hoping to see a doctor or a soldier or something. Who was this guy – and could he help us? Then I shook my head. Of course he would help. He was carrying a backpack, and he was risking his own neck to get to us.

I started running then, crashing through the bushes, scrambling up the bank toward him. The wind from the helicopter blasted down, like a huge hair dryer trying to rip the hair from my head.

The man reached the ground, landing between two straggly trees. He unclipped the rope and turned toward me. The helicopter lifted up and spun away. I stood watching it, scared it was going away, but it stayed, hovering above the river a little way downstream. I was so relieved that I started scrambling up the bank again.

"Easy, boy, easy!" the man cried, catching me as I threw myself at him. "It looks like you've had a little trouble here."

"It's my grandfather," I gasped. "He's in bad shape. I'm scared that…"

"It's okay," he said. "We're here now. You're not on your own anymore."

He jumped down the ridge then turned to give me a hand. "My name's Tony. I'm a paramedic. The pilot is Natalie, and we have a winchman on board named Ellis."

I plunged down the hill behind him, the noise of the helicopter pounding loudly in my head. "I'm Jim," I told him, "and Pa – my grandfather – is named William."

We got to the level ground. "What happened?" Tony asked, striding so quickly between the scrub and trees that I had to scramble to keep up.

I blurted out the story.

"How long was he under the water?" Tony snapped the question out.

"I don't know. It seemed like forever. And he hit his head. There was blood everywhere."

He looked down at me. "Don't worry, Jim. You've done your part. And it's been a mighty important part, too."

That wouldn't be a lot of comfort if Pa died.

We got to the tent. Tony ripped the pegs out and then gently pulled the tent away so that he could see Pa. "William? Can you hear me?" Pa murmured something. "My name's Tony. I'm a paramedic. We're going to get you to a hospital." He leaned over as Pa muttered something else. "It's okay. You're safe now."

He examined Pa carefully, starting at his head and working his way down. He took some scissors out of his pack and cut through the pieces of sleeping bag I'd used to splint Pa's leg. "Good work," he told me. "You did a nice job."

"Is he… will he…?" I couldn't bear to finish the question.

Tony tucked the sleeping bag back around Pa's body, leaving his leg exposed. "His blood pressure's pretty low, but it's not dangerous. They'll fix up his leg at the hospital. He's a little disoriented, but that's not surprising under the circumstances." He gave me a quick smile. "He should pull through. Is he a fighter?"

I looked at Pa. "Yes," I said, thinking about it. "Yes, he's a fighter. He's tough. He doesn't give up."

"That's the best thing he has going for him." Tony splinted the leg. "I'll strap his legs together to give him more support until we get him to the hospital." He worked quickly, never looking as if he wished he had an extra hand or two. "I can't figure out how you got him out of the river all by yourself. He must be six feet tall."

"Six foot two, actually," I said. And my father had been six two and a half.

Tony shook his head. "I don't know how you did it, Jim."

I gulped. "I had to. There was nobody else."

He put out a hand and gripped my shoulder for a second. "I'd take you fishing any day of the week."

I sat down slowly and watched. It was over, it was really over. I didn't have to worry anymore, or think, or decide things. It was weird, but all I wanted to do was collapse.

Tony reached into his pack again and brought out a radio. "Natalie, we need a stretcher here."

I looked over at the helicopter as it swooped back toward us. I could see the winchman waiting until they were above us, and then he lowered the stretcher to where Tony could unclip it from its line. Then the helicopter wheeled away again.

Tony put the stretcher beside Pa. "This is called a Stokes rescue basket," he said. "I'll get your grandfather into it, and then we'll cover him up, and strap everything down tight. It's going to get a little windy when we winch him up." He got Pa onto the stretcher without any effort at all. I thought of how I'd had to struggle and how hard it had been.

He took a silver blanket out of the pack and tucked it around Pa, then added another blanket, and finally strapped everything in place. He called the helicopter back. "Move away a little," he shouted to me. "The rotor wash is pretty fierce."

I took a few steps down the bank, but stayed where I could watch easily. Tony held four ropes that were attached to the stretcher and clipped them onto the winch line. Then he clipped his own harness to the line so that he was positioned where he could keep an eye on Pa as they went up.

It took maybe a minute. I watched the stretcher disappear into the helicopter, and then Tony came down again with a harness for me. He helped me put it on, clipped me to the line, and then steadied me as I was lifted off the ground.

Before I knew it, strong hands were helping me climb into the helicopter. Pa was still on his stretcher and the whole thing was strapped to the floor.

Ellis, the winchman, pointed to a seat behind the pilot. "Go ahead and grab a seat, Jim." He had to shout. I hadn't thought it would be so noisy. I strapped myself into the seat and Tony handed me

a headset. I put it on and heard Natalie's voice in my ears. "What happened, Jim?"

I told the story again.

They said nice things about how brave I'd been. I wished I felt like I'd been brave, but I didn't. I watched out the window. "It's a perfect day for flying," Natalie said. She pointed out a few landmarks. I saw the road where Grandma had dropped us. It didn't seem very far at all.

After a few minutes, Tony called up the hospital. I listened as he told them about Pa. The words swirled around in my head – fracture, blood pressure one hundred over sixty, concussion, conscious but some confusion. That was the part that really worried me.

Natalie said, "ETA fifteen minutes."

I looked at Ellis. "ETA?"

"Estimated time of arrival."

Oh. Of course.

We landed gently, and there was a man waiting with a gurney. They took Pa and put his stretcher on it. "Come with me," Tony said. "I'll help you get settled someplace until your family can get here."

Chapter Ten

I followed him as he wheeled Pa into the building. He showed me a waiting room. "You can hang out here, Jim. Somebody will be along soon to talk to you."

So I hung out, feeling very out of place in my dirty T-shirt, bare feet, and shorts. After about ten minutes, a woman with a clipboard came in and asked me questions about Pa, but I didn't know the answers to most of them. I wasn't even exactly sure how old he was – he was just Pa, always there, always big and solid, and always pretty annoyed at what a weakling of a grandson he had.

She went away to try to call Grandma. I sat and waited and wondered what I'd do if Grandma didn't turn up. What would I do if they couldn't find her? I couldn't even remember the name of the motel or the tiny town where we stayed.

I thought about Pa, too. Would he be okay? I put my head in my hands. I hoped he would be. I really hoped so. I'd found out that he really had guts. He was tough physically – sleeping on the bare ground sheet and all that stuff. But he was tough mentally, too – he hadn't complained once.

Would his mind come back? Or would he not know if I am myself or my father until he died?

Maybe I would have liked my father, after all. I felt a sudden stinging regret that I would never know. But at least now, I'd never hate him again. The fishing rod was still by the river, where the next flood would probably carry it away. That was a shame, but it didn't make me too sad. The picture I had of my father now was much more precious than his fishing rod.

I curled up on the seat and went to sleep. Then somebody was shaking me and hugging me and crying all at the same time. "Uh, hi, Grandma," I mumbled, trying to sit up.

"Jimmy!" she hiccuped and hugged me again.

"Is he going to be okay?" I sat up. Maybe that was why she was crying. Maybe after everything he'd been through, he'd died anyway.

"He's going to be fine, thanks to you." She wiped her eyes with a small tissue. "Oh, Jimmy, you were so brave and resourceful and smart!"

I'd really like a recording of that. It would sure come in handy the next time Pa got annoyed with me. "Have you talked to him?" I asked.

She shook her head. "No. They had to operate on his leg. He's still unconscious."

"Grandma," I said, not really wanting to say the next part, "he didn't know who I was a lot of the time. He thought I was Dad."

She gave me kind of a leaky smile. "Don't worry about it, Jimmy. They said he'll be fine. He had a concussion and a huge shock, but he's going to be completely fine."

She took me to stay with a friend of hers, and the next morning we went up to the hospital. I didn't want to go in. If Pa was still navigating by the wrong map, then I didn't think I could handle it. Grandma, however, wasn't worried. She just steamed into the room, hugged him, and started chattering away like a cage full of budgies.

I hung back behind her, out of his sight. She hadn't given him a chance to say anything, so I couldn't tell if he was okay or still on another planet. Then I heard his big rumbling voice – weaker than usual, but it still had quite a bit of bite

in it. "Louise, hush for a moment. Let me get a word in! Where's the boy?"

The boy. Which boy did he mean, me or Graham? "I'm right here, Pa." I walked up to the bed, holding my breath.

He reached out and took my hand. "You did a great job, son." His eyebrows twitched. "But I must say that I'm awfully glad I'm not a fish."

"Huh?" I stared at him. Maybe the odd marble was still floating around where it shouldn't be.

"Well, sure," he said in a sort of growl, "you'd have thrown me back if I were a fish!"

"Oh, Pa!" I groaned and collapsed onto the stool by his bed.

"Jimmy! It's all right," Grandma said, patting my head. "See, he's back to his old self, Jimmy."

"Listen, Louise," Pa said. "I think it's time we called him Jim. He's not a little kid anymore."

I just sat there, staring at him, my mouth half open. Pa wriggled his shoulders to get more comfortable on his pillows. "Yep, that's for sure. He's not a little kid." He shot me a glance from under his eyebrows. "I had to laugh, Jim, when I was down there by the river. I kept expecting you to say 'dig in, don't wait!' over my corpse. I thought about that a lot. It made me laugh."

I stared at him. "I wish..." I stopped. I couldn't tell him how I wished I'd known that he liked jokes.

He patted my hand. "I'm so proud of you, I could bust." He shut his eyes again.

Grandma stood up. "We'll come back later," she said. "He's still pretty tired."

I followed her out of the hospital, my head spinning.

People made a huge production out of how I rescued Pa. I got interviewed on television and radio, and a whole ton of reporters kept trying to talk to me.

Before long, I was pretty fed up with it all. I wondered what they'd say if I told the truth about how most of the time I'd been scared out of my mind and that all I'd wanted to do was lie down and give up. I talked to Pa about it three days after the rescue.

"Holy smoke, Jim, don't tell them that!" he said. "They'll make you into a saint instead of just a hero if you tell them all that stuff."

"But I want them to go away!" I groaned. "It really was no big deal. Anybody would have done the same."

"Listen, Jim," Pa said, knitting his eyebrows. "Give them what they want, and soon they'll find something else to get excited about. Then your face will be on the paper that's lining bird cages." He has a way of being strangely comforting – and he was right. By the time Mom flew back from Los Angeles on the fifth day after the accident, not one news place called her up to ask her about it.

Altogether, I only missed five days of school. John was green. "You are so lucky! Five days off school, a ride in a helicopter, and on top of everything else, you get your ugly mug plastered all over the television!"

"Yeah," I agreed. "And you should see what I've lined up for next month."

Pa had to stay in the hospital for a couple of weeks, and then Grandma borrowed a station wagon, shoved a mattress in the back of it, and drove him home. I went to visit him when I got home from school.

"How's it going, Pa?"

"I can't complain," he said. "I guess I still have a bit of life left in me." He was watching the baseball game, but he turned it off when I came in. That was something he'd never done before.

"Hey, Pa... Mrs. Cluny had that game on the radio during our last class. It sounded pretty tense. Can we watch it?" I felt sort of stupid, after all the times he'd tried to make me watch and I wouldn't.

He just gave me a long look. "I'd like that, Jim. I'd like that a lot." He switched it back on and we sat there. We really got into it – yelling and cheering and being a pair of couch umpires.

The game went into extra innings. "Not bad," Pa said when it was over. "Not bad at all."

I got up. "I'll see you soon, Pa. And I'm glad you're home."

I got to the door before he said, "Hey, Jim – I watched all the stuff on the rescue."

I turned around. "Oh? Well, I guess you weren't noticing a whole lot the first time around."

He waved a hand. "No. But the part that interested me was that cliff where you stuck the signal. It was a pretty tough climb."

"It wasn't too bad," I said. I knew how he felt about mountains and I couldn't blame him.

"I thought," he said slowly, "that when I'm on my feet again, I'd take you rock climbing. That is, if you want to go."

I stared at him. "But you always said… I mean, Dad died on a mountain…"

"Yes," he said. "He did. But that doesn't mean you will."

I was so astonished I couldn't move, couldn't talk, couldn't get out one of the excited words hurling around in my brain. Finally, I managed to yell, "Yes! Fantastic! Amazing! Awesome!" I stopped and looked at him, glancing at his leg and at the scar on his head.

"Yeah, I know, I know," he grumbled. "Getting hit on the head knocked some sense into me."

"I didn't say that," I said, grinning like an ape.

"You didn't have to," he said. "I can read you like a book." His eyes sparkled.

I ran home and I don't remember my feet touching the ground once. Good old Pa. So what if he could read me like a book – I'd learned quite a bit about reading him, too. For instance, I now knew that he was laughing when his eyes sparkled. I was so glad that he hadn't died. But I still didn't think I'd risk showing him my spelling or asking him to come skateboarding with me. He'd probably need a few more knocks to the head before he thought both of those were all right. But it's funny, I don't seem to mind that anymore.

I teach in a junior high school and write during weekends and vacations. It's great being a teacher and a writer. I can try out my books on the students I teach, and if I have a bad day at school, I can come home and create a world where everybody does exactly what I want them to! I have two grown daughters and a cat that rules the household.

Fleur Beale

I'm a second-generation native of Colorado. I have loved creating artwork all my life. I live in Golden, Colorado, with my wife, Rebecca, and our blended family of Nicolle, Paul, Matt, and Megan. I'd like to thank my son Paul and my best man, Milt Presler, who helped with the illustrations by becoming the two main characters and acting out their precarious predicaments. I couldn't have done it without them.

Shawn Shea

That's a Laugh

Queen of the Bean
Cinderfella's Big Night
The Flying Pig and the Daredevil Dog
Ants Aren't Antisocial
Charlotte's Web Page
Playing with Words

Thrills and Spills

Mountain Bike Mania
Destination Disaster
Journey to the New World
The Secret of Bunratty Castle
Happy Accidents!
The Chocolate Flier

Challenges and Choices

Call of the Selkie
Trailblazers!
The Hole in the Hill
The Good, the Bad,
    and Everything Else
On the Edge
The Willow Pattern

Our Wild World

Isn't It Cool? Discovering Antarctica
    and the Arctic
The Horse, of Course
Trapped by a Teacher
Mystery Bay
The Rain Forest
Feathery Fables

© Text by **Fleur Beale**
Illustrated by **Shawn Shea**
Edited by **Rebecca McEwen**
Designed by **Karen Baxa Hoglund**

04 03 02 01 00
10 9 8 7 6 5 4 3 2

Distributed in the United States by
    RIGBY
    a division of Reed Elsevier Inc.
    P.O. Box 797
    Crystal Lake, IL 60039-0797

Printed in Hong Kong.
ISBN: 0-7699-0419-X